*To all the
good friends of
Miss Bilberry*

ACROSS T·H·E BLUE MOUNTAINS

Emma Chichester Clark

Gulliver Books

Harcourt Brace & Company

San Diego   New York   London

Miss Bilberry lived in a pale yellow house at the base of the great blue mountains with a dog named Cecilie, a cat called Chester, and two birds called Chitty and Chatty.

Every morning Miss Bilberry had breakfast in the shade of a broad-leaved tree, looking out at her beautiful view of the mountains.

After breakfast she swept the path and fed the birds and animals.
She watered the flowers and vegetables growing in her garden.
Then she had a light lunch on the veranda.

In the afternoon she had a nap in her hammock between two sway-ing palms. And sometimes in the evening she played her violin and sang a few songs before she went to bed.

It was a lovely life, and Miss Bilberry would have been completely happy, except for one thing.

She just couldn't stop wondering whether she might not be even happier if she lived on the other side of the mountains. The more she looked, the more she wondered.

One day, Miss Bilberry could stand it no longer. "Everybody up!" she called to Cecilie, Chester, and Chitty and Chatty. "Today's the day! We're going to move! Let's start packing!"

Not wanting to be left behind, they all helped fill boxes, baskets, and bags and put everything from the little yellow house onto a wobbly old cart.

Then they waved good-bye to the house and the garden, the broad-leaved tree and the two swaying palms, and set off toward the blue mountains.

"I just can't wait to get to the other side!" cried Miss Bilberry. But Chester looked back sadly.

They walked and walked, pushing the heavy cart for many miles, through fields,

and forests,

through rain,

and sunshine,

uphill,

and downhill.

On and on they went.

Chester grumbled, Cecilie moaned, but Miss Bilberry just kept going.

And there it was . . .

"Oh my!" gasped Miss Bilberry. "It's perfection. It's just as I thought it would be!"

"Thank goodness for that," sighed Chester.

Chester and Cecilie ran the rest of the way. When Miss Bilberry caught up they all unpacked the boxes and emptied the bags. In between loads Chester sniffed the air. It's strange, he thought, but I feel as if I've been here before.

Miss Bilberry was so tired that she slept all afternoon in her hammock, which she strung between two swaying palms, exactly as before. Then she made a stew from the vegetables growing in the garden, and they all began to feel better.

Each morning when the sun shone in her window, Miss Bilberry leapt out of bed. Her life seemed better than ever. Her breakfast seemed more delicious and the mountains seemed more beautiful.

It was a lovely life and she was happy. But there were some things that bothered Miss Bilberry . . .

. . . she didn't say anything, but she just couldn't stop wondering.

It seemed to her that even though they had traveled a very long way, everything was much the same. Even the mountains, which should really have been at the back of the house, were still in front. It was a mystery to Miss Bilberry, and she sometimes worried about it.

Chester, the clever cat, smiled to himself. He knew the answer, but he would never tell Miss Bilberry. He liked their quiet life in the pale yellow house with its broad-leaved tree, its two swaying palms, and its cool veranda.